# AVA
## *and the*
# BIG OUCH
## A BOOK ABOUT FEELING BETTER

By Lucy Bell

Illustrated by Michael Garton

First edition published 2018
Printed in the United States
23 22 21 20 19 18     1 2 3 4 5 6 7 8

Hardcover ISBN: 978-1-5064-2504-7

Illustrated by Michael Garton
Designed by Tim Palin

Library of Congress Control Number: 2017954765

Sparkhouse Family
510 Marquette Avenue
Minneapolis, MN 55402
sparkhouse.org

SPARK
HOUSE
FAMILY
sparkhousefamily.org

Ava loved to scamper and play with her friends.

She liked to run as fast as she could through the grass. She liked to cross the stream by leaping from stone to stone.

But most of all, Ava liked to climb the big tree.

She liked to climb up the trunk. She liked to look down at how small everything looked from the big branch. And she loved to use the vine to swing back to the ground.

But one day, when Ava was climbing
the big tree, her hoof slipped.

Ava lost her balance.

She fell off the branch and hit the ground hard!

Her knee had a big ouch. She cried and cried.

"Are you okay, Ava?" Hal asked.
Ava shook her head.

"I'll help you up, Ava," Rufus said.
Ava shook her head.

She didn't want to get up.

"Come run with me, Ava!" Hal said.

"Come skip across the river with me, Ava!"
Rufus called out.

But Ava shook her head again.

Ava didn't feel like running. She didn't feel like skipping. And she never wanted to climb a tree or swing from a vine ever again.

Ava didn't want to play anymore.
She wanted to go home.

"Won't you play with us?" Hal asked.

"Do you want to climb the tree?" Rufus asked.
"That's your favorite!"

But Ava wouldn't go.

"I don't want to fall down again."

"What if I climb the tree with you?"
Rufus asked, "Then will you go?"

Ava thought about it. But she was afraid she might fall again.

"What if I stand at the bottom?" Hal asked,
"Then I could catch you if you fall."

Ava thought about it some more.
But she was still afraid.

"I just don't want to get hurt again."
Ava told her friends. "The last time I climbed
the tree, I fell down and got a big ouch!"

"Don't give up, Ava!" Hal cried.

"You should try the tree again," Rufus said. "You still want to have fun, don't you?"

Ava nodded. She *did* still want to have fun. And her big ouch was starting to feel a little better. But the big tree suddenly looked very, very high.

Ava closed her eyes.

Dear God,

Getting hurt doesn't feel very good. But I know you're with me even when I'm hurt. Help me to be brave.

Amen.

Ava climbed up the trunk very carefully.

She inched out onto the big branch.

Then she grabbed the vine and swung down to the ground. She giggled as she sailed through the air, then landed safely on the ground.

Rufus and Hal ran up to Ava.

"You did it, Ava!" they cheered.

Ava blushed. She was so proud of herself!

"Let's do it again!" she said.
"Race you to the top!"

## ABOUT THE STORY

Ava loves to play, but after she gets hurt, she's suddenly afraid to return to one of her favorite activities. Can her friends, and a prayer, help her have fun again?

## DELIGHT IN READING TOGETHER

As you read this story, ask your child if they've ever gotten hurt like Ava, and how they reacted. Were they scared? Just as Ava overcomes her fear of getting hurt, your child can learn that they don't have to be afraid of experiencing life, even after "big ouches" happen!

## DEVELOPMENT CONNECTION

Different children respond to getting hurt differently. Some kids will bounce back right away, while others will want to cling to you for a while before they're ready to get back out there. Knowing your child, you'll know best whether they should take it easy or if they need a gentle nudge to start playtime again.

## FAITH CONNECTION

We get hurt sometimes, and don't always know why. But we know that God is with us in our pain, and wants to heal us. God's love is with us when we hurt.

*He heals the brokenhearted and binds up their wounds.*
        *Psalm 147:3*

## SAY A PRAYER

Say the prayer Ava said when she was sad about getting hurt.

*Dear God, Getting hurt doesn't feel very good. But I know you're with me even when I'm hurt. Help me to be brave.*

*Amen.*

**xxx**

## NIGHT SONG

*Chiljilt, sichizi, gunjule, inzayu, ijanale.*
— Apache prayer

At dawn, I found Dragonfly dying
Beside my path, far from water,
His blue needle stitching breath
To breath, catching at air
With the dry nets of his wings.
Now I lie by the same path, my fear
Beside me in darkness, breathing.
*Night, be good, do not let me die.*

At noon, in a circle of stones, I found
The breath-feather of Hawk.
He has fallen somewhere
To the mouths of his smallest brothers
Who will crawl out of the cracked earth
To steal his eyes, to take him
Where he has never flown before.
*Night, be good, do not let me die.*

At evening, West Wind fell.
Sun fell. Sky closed again.
The sharp small spilled water-filled song
Of Wren went dry as my mouth.
The open yellow-and-white hands
Of Cactus Woman gathered to fists.
Now the fire's heart shrinks like my heart.
*Night, be good, do not let me die.*

�✗

# Three

## FINDING THE RIGHT DIRECTION

Those times when too much stands between you and the sky —
Tree crowns and clouds or mist — when the hidden sun
Makes nothing of your shadow
To guide you south, you turn to stones, to slopes and trees,
To flowers, even to birds for your directions:
Cutting across bedrock,
The scars of glacial drift all point the same hard way
To mark the graveyard of ice which trundled boulders
Grindingly up hills
And, gouging abrupt drop-offs, tumbled them over and over
And left them strewn like markers, blunt in smooth fields,
While it melted south
On one straight, glittering journey which you may follow now
Rejoicing toward the end of your own ice age,
Sunbound and shrinking,
Or if the brush grows dense and your unmindful eyes
Can't choose between the dextrous and sinister,
See, the lightest branches,
The thickest, hardest bark most deeply grooved, the heaviest
Roots of old trees will stand to the bitter north,
Braced against winter,
And even the newly dead will show where not to go:
The center of decay lies out of sunlight.
Young trees lean *with* you
Like the new grass in this clearing where you've stumbled, seeing
Wildflowers sharing your clouds, but staring southward
For the certain return
Of what once brought them to light and, look, this empty cabin

At the edge of it, unhinged by years of weather,
Has under the southern eaves
Your surest compass, expecting a break in the gray of morning:
A swallow's nest clinging to next to nothing
Like you, beginning now.

## WALKING IN BROKEN COUNTRY

Long after the blossoming of mile-wide, fire-breathing roses
In this garden of dead gods when Apache tears
Burst out of lava
And after the crosshatched lightning and streambeds cracking
Their sideslips through mid-rock, after burnishing wind,
Your feet are small surprises:
Lurching down clumps of cinders, unpredictably slipshod,
And gaining your footholds by the sheerest guesswork,
You make yourself at home
By crouching, by holding still and squinting to puzzle out
How to weave through all this rubble to where you're going
Without a disaster:
One dislocation, one green-stick fracture, and all your bones
May fall apart out of sympathy forever.
In this broken country
The shortest distance between two points doesn't exist.
Here, straight lines are an abstraction, an ideal
Not even to be hoped for
(As a crow flies, sometimes) except on the briefest of terms:
Half a step on legs, after which you slump,
Swivel, or stagger.
You cling to surfaces feebly in a maze without a ceiling,
A whole clutch of directions to choose among
From giddy to earthbound,
Where backtracking from dead-ends is an end in itself.
Through this clear air, your eyes put two and two
Together, take them apart,

And put them together again and again in baffling pieces,
Seeing the matter of all your sensible facts
Jumbled to the horizon.

**✖✖✖**

*CLIMBING  ALONE*


Against your own judgment, you begin climbing these rocks,
Using your grudging, shaky extremities
For footholds and handholds
In a school of hard knocks where kneecaps, crazybones, skull,
Even coccyx, demand your strictest attention:
They must take new postures
Slowly and surely enough to keep your center of gravity
From getting above itself and joining rock slides.
The joys of mass wasting
In the wrong direction are better left to minerals
At which you stare up close, highly concerned
With their good health,
Their age and strength, their disposition, their failures,
And the likelihood of their remaining with you
When you cling to them.
You don't look down or back: for the purposes of falling,
A little distance is as good as a mile.
It goes a long, long way
To nowhere, putting your body permanently out of condition.
You brace up a chimney, right-angled, steeping yourself
In the history of stress,
But when you stop to think or breathe, as you must, to perform
The necessary functions of not fainting
And not losing your mind,
Your best intentions seem more ludicrous than usual.
At the height of your foolishness you remember why
On earth you wanted to do this

And find it unfathomably strange, seeing coiled beside you
Your rope with nothing at the end of it
But the end of it.

**⚹⚹⚹**

## CROSSING A RIVER

You kneel on the verge of this impassable arroyo,
Filled now with a river instead of easy dust,
And drink it in
Literally, pumice and all, not from the sealed lips
Of your canteen but, to celebrate, from your hands,
And watch it surging
Between you and the impossible place you had meant to go,
Past a stream like a stairway, flooded and broken
At the foot of a monument
To the greater glory of stones, all cutbanks and no point bars,
A torrent not to be forded if you can't stand
The equal partnership
Of branches, rocks, and whole bushes, its leapfrogging bedload,
Which would carry you off and lose you without a murmur.
You could sit down
And eventually it would dwindle, falter, and go away
Like a second thought failing before your eyes,
Or you could climb,
Maybe, scraping your way up cliffs to its source, finding nothing,
No fountainhead to circle and mull around
Or to turn young by,
Just seasonally bad weather running off cloudy spillways.
So you head downstream on the good side of it,
Trying to get somewhere
The way *it* does: temporarily. This scarred, unearthly ravine
May be someone's, and the fullness thereof, but not yours,
Not even this river's
For long, as it makes up its mind about the weakness

Of what lies under it, what to carry away,
What course to choose
While glancing toward gravity, making no grand progress
And not resounding through multi-colored canyons
But disappearing
Abruptly with all its rainwash in a flattening fan
In the dry silt of the playa beside you
Where, if you've played along,
You'll find your eyes intent on a different level, not broken
Yet, where water goes underground without you.
Here you are free to cross.

**✳✳✳**

## STANDING IN THE MIDDLE OF A DESERT

You stop halfway in this bleakness to reconsider
Everything underfoot,
Which, like white sunlight and the punishing air,
Seems in favor of dying.
You don't have enough essential qualities
To vegetate here:
You may be distorted, bitter, fleshy, and smooth,
But not well armored,
Not deeply or widely rooted, gray-green, or dwarfish.
An executioner
Like that crook-backed creosote whose poisonous roots
Kill its own seedlings
(Unless some unlikely rain leaches the earth)
Has one idea: its life.
But if you stayed still and tried to be self-effacing,
You'd bear numberless offspring
Whose sincerest flattery wouldn't be imitation
But helping themselves to you:
They'd be overjoyed to live on your behalf,
Leave nothing to waste,
Leave nothing at all to your imagination,
So you have to move,
Marking your time in this intractable sand,
More footloose than ever.

**✖✖✖**

## AT THE POINT OF NO RETURN

Till now, you could have taken back your steps
Like slips of the foot:
They were turning points where, more easily than not,
You could have given up,
Gone back to the start, forgotten, tried something different.
But from here on
It will take more courage to turn than to keep going.
You take two strides,
Each boot on its own, and you're headed one way only,
Irresponsibly committed,
Refreshed by the absence of the power to choose.
You enjoy believing
Your tracks in the blowing sand (that dusty mulch
Protecting deeper water)
May offer for an hour thousands of shelters,
Small rooting places
For seeds that, without you, would have kept on tumbling
Unfulfilled downwind,
So your line of march, no matter how misdirected
By your fixed or wandering
Star-sighted, red-rimmed eyes, may be remembered
By an equally erratic,
Interrupted, and inexplicable line of survivors,
Which till their last season
Will be straining root and branch taller than dunes
To postpone their burial.

## LIVING OFF THE LAND

Your eyes gnaw at the land ahead for food. You travel
Light-headed, ravenous, your jaws rehearsing
Zigzagging ruminations,
Grindings, incisive choppings, those broad-minded habits
That make you omnivorous by reputation
But in name only:
Here, in the desert, your natural disadvantages
Come into focus better than your eyes —
A rank amateur's nose,
A lack of teeth ridged well enough for the mangling of thorns,
Shortness of daily range, shortness of breath,
The griping of your guts
At the half-thought of settling for carrion like the vultures
Now effortlessly hanging-fire around you,
Concerned for your welfare.
You know what coyotes know: sheep may not safely graze
With or without a shepherd near your hunger.
But being a scavenger
Means learning to skulk till carcasses and the time seem ripe.
The relative deadness of flesh depends on timing
As much as taste
Unfortunately for you, whose hungry, impatient ancestors
Survived (in a world where bones grew popular)
By being and tasting terrible:
At best, you would be last in line at communal dinners
Under this meat-loving sun, or the last of your line
At the dead head of it.
If you look under your feet, whose shrinking, hardening shadows

Match every step you take, burnt black by sunlight,
You see you could grub there
Or grovel for one more grubstake, kneeling, praying for seeds
(If any nearby have had decent burial)
To sprout and bear fruit,
But for you it's a waiting game that might take generations
To master: all the lost seasons, all the clouds
That never arrive
Except in their own good time, when you, having drifted off,
Might not remember what every seed remembers:
What it is.
You'd have turned into all you can eat, this air and this sand,
Faltering, flowing even without water
Uneventfully downwind.

## READING THE LANDSCAPE

You sit and breathe, scanning the raw illusions of distance
And nearness for the lay of this land, depending
On what you are,
A pivot casting the only restless shadow for miles.
Far off, the horizon traces its own downfall —
Mountainous once,
The wrack of living seas, steep fire, a storming of stones,
Now slowly settling for less under the weather,
That fearless explorer
Of weakness in the bindings of mind and matter. Nearby, lost ice
Through freeze and thaw has cracked a granite causeway
Where gnarled manzanita
Has made one fault its own, has wrestled for root-room,
And now bears fruit you share with unknown neighbors.
You feel strangely at home
In the visible world, a place called Here and There, on the seat
Of kings, the gluteus maximus, deluded
Into thinking you're not lost
At the heart of this bewilderment. Your only shelters
Are half-shut eyes and a shut mouth, but sandgrains
(Once firm rock, now shattered)
Have entered those three rooms, sharing your misunderstandings
Of what you say and see, reminding you
Your mind's voice and mind's eye
Are equally vulnerable in their pastimes and desolations,
Their taste for all the flavors of light and shade
And the sweet nothings
Of casual, elaborate, or desperate speech. Your duties

Are to rest and be recreated, then to stand,
Ignoring all directions
But your own, and to exercise your freedom of chance by aiming
Somewhere, keeping a constant Here beside you
As faithfully as your death.

## SEEING THINGS

Browbeaten by the sun,
Squinting, and long since out of focus yourself
In a sharp-edged, keen-eyed world, you take whatever looms
Or lords it over you
Or spills its rippling lakes across this desert
More placidly than those expecting to feel cold sober.
You know that shimmer of water
Isn't for you, will keep a critical distance
Like grazing antelope sidling from your approaches.
You know that heavenly mansion
Hanging upside down or having it both ways
To a pinnacle is a shack or boulder beyond the horizon
Where you would spend hard times.
You know the delectable mountains like layer cakes
Are twice as far away as they seem and completely inedible.
But your fondness for light,
For the earth's unlimited metamorphoses,
Should help you go along with its disguises, shifting
(But not uneasily)
The burden of proof to the eyes of other beholders
Who don't know what you are, who may be seeing you now
As a menacing, blurred afrit,
A towering apparition wobbling toward them
Helplessly, their last hope, their disillusionment.

✖✖✖

## LYING AWAKE IN A DESERT

Displaced by darkness, you lie flat on your back,
Putting the world behind you, and stare at the moon,
The embarrassing moon, with nothing to offer it,
No ebb or flow, no wolfish transformations
Except this lunacy you keep to yourself.

You feel defenseless at last — no choice of weapons
And no opponent, only a field of honor,
This sand where you make little or no impression,
Though it takes you as you are, dead or alive,
As a kind of minor natural disaster.

If a sound should startle you out of your unsound sleep,
Whistling, buzzing, or droning, wingbeats, scuttling
Of small dry claws, lie still. Nothing at night
Makes noise by accident. If you hear, you were meant to
Or the indifferent source has found you harmless.

No matter how cold you feel to yourself, your colleagues —
The scorpions, sidewinders, and spiny swifts —
Will come to share the benefit of your body
And its residual heat. They'll lie beside you
More trustingly than you could with a stranger.

So if you wake in the morning, do it gently,
One eye, one branch, one thought, one stretch at a time,
Being a homing place and point of departure.
Meanwhile, get through this night of reckoning
By the irrational riches of starlight.

**xxx**

## LOOKING FOR WATER

At the lip of your canteen, kissing that last sure drop
Goodbye, you choose the least unlikely direction —
Hills (if there are any)
Or greenness (if there is such a shade) or somewhere familiar
(If you can remember how some map unfolded
For your civilized fingers
By artificial light) — or barring those choices, anywhere.
You're keeping cool in spite of the persuasions
Of the surrounding air,
The parched ground burning underfoot, the sun too thirsty
Now that you're living by the sweat of your brow.
You watch for clouds
Like a furrow-faced, drought-plagued farmer ready to hire
The dry wits of witches, cannons of rainmakers,
Or prayers made of sand.
Though they make no streambed for that smallest of tributaries
Under your tongue, you put small stones in your mouth
For their durable comfort
But, with what remains of your breath, practice no oratory
Here in this speechless country, wasting no words
On self-absorbed cacti:
Though you behead one, crush its pale pulpy heart, squeeze out
Briefly what it had saved through fifty summers,
And leave it dying,
Your graying stubble drains off no excess heat like its needles,
And your blundering, rootless sense of territory
Can't match its self-possession.
You may find, by growing or fading light, a waterhole

With genuine liquid filling a charmed circle
Before your very knees,
But if nothing green surrounds it, one slip of the tongue,
One head-first impulse, and you may leave yourself
In a roofless mortuary,
Yet if suddenly real bushes are offering real leaves
Or if at the foot of a hill you find seep willows
Or anything blooming
In a dry creekbed or lakebed, or if you can listen hard,
Not to the ragged pulse in your mind's ear
(That deserted music)
For the actual droning of bees, for actual birdsong, and can follow
To the place where they've made their lives over and over,
Where deer-flies hover
Green and gold above damp sand or clay, start digging.
Wait by that emptiness. If it trickles and fills,
Your luck is only beginning.
The flies and bees will join you in that bitter communion,
Will take it with you, as drunk as true believers
Sharing another kingdom.

**✖✖✖**

## GETTING THERE

You take a final step and, look, suddenly
You're there. You've arrived
At the one place all your drudgery was aimed for:
This common ground
Where you stretch out, pressing your cheek to sandstone.
What did you want
To be? You'll remember soon. You feel like tinder
Under a burning glass,
A luminous point of change. The sky is pulsing
Against the cracked horizon,
Holding it firm till the arrival of stars
In time with your heartbeats.
Like wind etching rock, you've made a lasting impression
On the self you were
By having come all this way through all this welter
Under your own power,
Though your traces on a map would make an unpromising
Meandering lifeline.
What have you learned so far? You'll find out later,
Telling it haltingly
Like a dream, that lost traveller's dream
Under the last hill
Where through the night you'll take your time out of mind
To unburden yourself
Of elements along elementary paths
By the break of morning.
You've earned this worn-down, hard, incredible sight

Called Here and Now.
Now, what you make of it means everything,
Means starting over:
The life in your hands is neither here nor there
But getting there,
So you're standing again and breathing, beginning another
Journey without regret
Forever, being your own unpeaceable kingdom,
The end of endings.

## ✖✖✖

# ACKNOWLEDGMENTS

Some of the poems in this volume have been previously published in the following: *American Poetry Review* ("Finding the Right Direction"), *Antaeus* ("Thawing a Birdbath on New Year's Day"), *The Atlantic* ("Part Song," "Ode to the Muse on Behalf of a Young Poet," "Lament for the Non-swimmers," "Pile-driver," "Return to the River"), *Blue Buildings* ("At the Edge of a Clear-cut Forest," "Getting There"), *Carolina Quarterly* ("To the Fly in My Drink"), *Chicago Review* ("Cloudburst," "Meditation on the Union Bay Garbage Fill"), *Field* ("Into the Nameless Places"), *The Georgia Review* ("Climbing Alone"), *Graham House Review* ("For a Woman Who Said Her Soul Was Lost"), *Hampden-Sydney Poetry Review* ("Standing in the Middle of a Desert," "At the Point of No Return"), *Hudson Review* ("Love Song After a Nightmare," "Book Sale — Five Cents Each!"), *Kayak* ("Stunts"), *Massachusetts Review* ("Making a Fire in the Rain," "Living Off the Land"), *The New Yorker* ("My Father's Wall," "Seeds," "Sitting by a Swamp"), *Ohio Review* ("Walking in Broken Country"), *Oregon East* ("Looking Up"), *Paris Review* ("The Junior Highschool Band Concert"), *Poetry* ("Thistledown," "Elegy While Pruning Roses," "The Death of the Moon," "The Gift," "Elegy for a Minor Romantic Poet," "Being Herded Past the Prison's Honor Farm," "To a Panhandler Who, for a Quarter, Said 'God Bless You'," "After Reading Too Many Poems, I Watch a Robin Taking a Bath," "Cutting Down a Tree," "Crossing a River," "Seeing Things"), *Poetry in the Cities: Snohomish County Arts Council* ("Night Song"), *Poetry Miscellany* ("An Address to Weyerhaeuser, the Tree-growing Company," "Buck Fever," "Duck-blind"), *Portland Review* ("The Singers"), *Prairie Schooner* ("Songs My Mother Taught Me," "Watching the Harbor Seals," "For a Woman Who Dreamed All the Horses Were Dying"), *Raccoon* ("Epitaphs"), *Salmagundi* ("Reading the Landscape," "Lying Awake in a Desert"), *Shenandoah* ("Judging Logs"), *Southern Review* ("Trapline"), *Times Literary Supplement* ("Boy Jesus," "Setting a Snare," "Posing with a Trophy," "The Orchard of the Dreaming Pigs," "Looking for Water"), *Western Humanities Review* ("After the Speech to the Librarians," "Jeremiad," "Dirge for a Player-piano," "My Flying Circus," "Waterfall," "Shadow").